My Magic Wand

Written by
Karen Hoenecke

Illustrated by
Mark Hoenecke

Little Star Books

I can wave my wand.
It sparkles in the air.

Poof!

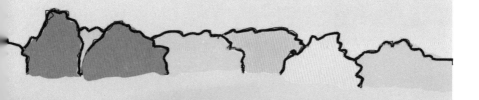

POOF! I see something
. . .fluffy.
What do you think is there?

A bunny!

I can wave my wand.
It sparkles in the air.

POOF! I see something
. . .squeaky.
What do you think is there?

A mouse!

I can wave my wand.
It sparkles in the air.

6

POOF! I see something
. . .heavy.
What do you think is there?

A rock!

I can wave my wand.
It sparkles in the air.

POOF! I see something
. . .singing.
What do you think is there?

I can wave my wand.
It sparkles in the air.

POOF! I see something
...round.
What do you think is there?

A ball!

I can wave my wand.
It sparkles in the air.

POOF! I see something
. . .cold.
What do you think is there?

An ice cream cone!

I can wave my wand.
It sparkles in the air.

POOF! I see something
. . .colorful.
What do you think is there?

A rainbow, balloons and flowers!